Submissive fantasy

Domination and erotic submission

Erika Sanders

Submissive fantasy

Erika Sanders

Serie

Domination and erotic submission

Synopsis

I took a deep breath and slowly blew it out, licking my dry lips.

Had he only been in control for an hour?

Or at least the option to walk away?

I heard him moving around the room, the TV turning back on ... realizing he was waiting for me to get comfortable.

I closed my eyes, not that it mattered since I couldn't see through the blindfold anyway ...

Submissive fantasy is a story with strong erotic BDSM content and, in turn, also belonging to the Erotic Domination collection, a series of novels with high romantic and erotic BDSM content.

Index:

SUBMISSIVE FANTASY

ERIKA SANDERS

"Now you've really gotten yourself into a bind."

I snorted softly.

It was a very unladylike sound, but for the moment, all I could think about was what would happen next.

Had he really read between the lines of all our emails?

From online chats?

From the late-night phone calls?

Perhaps it should have been more subtle.

That's what all the magazines say, right?

Guys need me to tell them what to do.

"Relax, Debbie."

The whisper against my ear made me jump.

"Easy for you to say, Harry."

"Shh. I'll be back."

I took a deep breath and slowly blew it out, licking my dry lips.

Had he only been in control for an hour?

Or at least the option to walk away?

I heard him moving around the room, the TV turning back on ... realizing he was waiting for me to get comfortable.

I closed my eyes, not that it mattered, as I couldn't see through the blindfold anyway, and I thought about earlier tonight ...

CHAPTER II

I picked up my cell phone and exhaled.

My finger hovered over the SEND button, my eyes glued to the two words on the screen: I'm HERE.

I took a deep breath and sealed my fate, praying that my nerves would calm down, that I no longer felt nauseous.

There was no going back now.

The sound of a toilet flushing drowned out the sound of a nearby phone.

An instant later, the door in front of me opened and my nerves were magnified.

"Are you going to stand there all night?" He said quiet.

The deep voice came from the lighted door.

Harry

I no longer had to close my eyes to imagine it.

His broad shoulders protruded a foot above me, wrapped in a button-down shirt with the sleeves rolled up to the elbows.

His obsidian eyes stared into mine with a brilliant gaze.

His big hands gripping the frame and door as he leaned down the hall toward me.

Our last and first meeting had been at a gangster and cabaret themed dance a week earlier.

My own terrain, my own friends, my own comfort zone.

It had been easy to fall in love with her charms, the way she hugged me when we danced slowly.

The way he tipped my felt hat into the parking lot before kissing me softly, his fingers barely touching my cheek.

The way he'd whispered in my ear that my decision to dress gangster had turned him on.

My knees buckled as he pressed against my hip, showing his arousal.

It took all my strength that I can get out of myself for the next seven days, especially at work.

Our late-night chats on the phone and on the Internet did not help.

So why was she so scared?

I was indulging in the moment that I had been fantasizing all this time ...

"Debbie?" She opened the door and stepped fully out into the hall now, the corners of her mouth down. "Are you okay?"

I backed against the wall, clutching my evening bag over my shoulder.

It's a mistake.

I shouldn't have come.

What was I thinking?

Wait, I wasn't thinking.

Me ...

His fingers brushed my cheek as he lifted my chin.

"Okay. Don't be afraid."

"Who me?" My voice sounded shaky and not at all confident, although I smiled.

His frown deepened.

Worry and disappointment showed in his dark eyes.

"Don't you want to do this?"

"Yes. I'll be fine."

I backed away from the wall, marching toward the lion's den.

The door slammed shut behind me, making me jump as I took in the surroundings.

It was a standard hotel room with a Jacuzzi bath to the left, the clothes rail in an alcove to the right, and an open-front suite with two lamps and a digital clock on small tables flanking the single bed.

A sofa, table, two chairs, and a low dresser with a television screwed on top of it finished off the furniture.

Uncool.

But then, it wasn't a special occasion.

Well, not one that you would rent a luxury hotel room for, like for a honeymoon.

A soft snort escaped my last thought.

No, nothing important like that.

There was a tug on my arm and I blinked.

My eyes lifted to meet his, and his soft smile eased the tension a bit.

"Let me take your bag."

I released my grip on the strap, watching him place the duffel bag on the dresser below the lit but silent TV screen.

He pressed a button on the remote control and the screen went black.

Now it was really just the two of us.

The little sounds now seemed amplified.

The soft hiss of the air conditioning unit.

The hum of light above our heads.

The noise of ice in the machine right outside the room.

The gurgling of water in the corner Jacuzzi next to the bed.

Well, maybe this isn't such a standard hotel room after all.

My heart was beating in my ears.

I tried to keep my breathing even, tried to focus on the whole situation.

In what he was doing.

Why he was doing it.

A soft moan escaped me as I thought of the possible end result, and something clenched in my gut.

"Debbie? Sit down."

He took my hand and led me to the bed.

My skin tingled from the contact.

My knees buckled automatically, and then I was resting on the edge.

My short stature made it difficult for me to sit up and still be able to touch the carpet.

"You look beautiful tonight."

I blinked again and tilted my head towards him.

No one had ever called me beautiful except my parents.

Her eyes focused on the dress she had chosen for the dance tonight, a red silk skirt with a rose print and a black sleeveless bodice that provided a wide neckline.

It was one of my favorites, mainly because I felt beautiful, despite my small body.

A smile drew my lips, glad that he would have liked it too.

"I-I'm sorry. I'm just a little ..."

"It's fine I understand it". He sat next to me, still holding my hand.

For several minutes, the only noise we made was our breathing, his normal, mine staggered.

How can you be so calm?

I kept my gaze on my lap, swallowing heavily as when I wandered onto his lap ... I saw the slight bulge there.

He would squeeze my hand from time to time.

Finally, when I felt calm, I raised my eyes to his face.

He was looking at me.

The corners of his mouth were now turned up.

"I'm going to kiss you, okay?"

I tilted my chin in response, and then his hand cupped my jaw, pulling me closer.

My eyes closed when his warm lips touched mine.

They touched lightly at first and then they pushed me harder.

I squeezed his hand, sucking in air, little shrieks of surprise reaching my ears.

His hand slid to the back of my head, his fingers buried in the strands of my hair.

When his tongue drew my mouth, I winced.

When he bit my lower lip, I gasped.

And when his tongue slid inside, shaking my tongue, I groaned.

Harry continued to hold my mouth with his until our tongues danced, savoring each other, and my moans became more frequent.

He pulled his hand out of mine and released the clip that was holding my chestnut ripples.

The gentle waves cascaded over my shoulders, whispering against my ears and cheeks before I pushed them away so I could hold my head more firmly.

My hand found his thigh and squeezed it, eliciting a groan from him.

Our bodies turned against each other, nerves softening as he helped me slide onto the quilt.

When I leaned back against the pillows, I sighed and anticipation replaced the anxiety in my tense muscles.

His fingers caressed my cheeks and my forehead and neck, twisting through my braids as he moved his mouth against mine.

He was gentle but firm.

In control, but not in a hurry either.

My fingers lifted to trace the contours of her neck, through the light stubble on her jaw, to her wavy hair, supporting her head.

When his fingers slid to my shoulder, over the wide strap of my dress bodice, and brushed my bare arm, I held my breath in my mouth.

Even through her dress and bra, she could feel the warmth of her touch.

I longed for him to take my chest, to ease a bit of the pressure I'd been feeling since we met.

It was so close, but it seemed to be avoiding that area on purpose.

"You taste so good." His mouth covered mine once more before moving to my chin, jaw, and behind my ear before settling into the curve of my neck.

His nose caressed me, his tongue licking my flesh.

I took a deep breath and let it out slowly with a groan.

"You smell amazing."

I whimpered, my skin tingling as he ravaged her.

"Please don't stop. Mmm."

"I have no intention of doing it." His voice was muffled as he sucked gently, nibbled, and then licked with the resulting sharp pains.

I grabbed his arms, anchoring myself to him.

His warm body pressed against my side, igniting sparks under my skin.

I wanted to put it on top of me, but I just didn't have the energy.

Or the guts to take the initiative.

His mouth landed butterfly kisses on my shoulder and down my throat.

When he left, I opened my eyes.

His eyes were fixed, but not on my face.

I continued on her way, and gasped when I saw the object of her concentration: the rapid rise and fall of my breasts pushing against the limits of the neckline of the dress.

My gaze returned to his face just in time to see him lick his lips.

"If you want me to stop, now would be the time ..."

"No no no". I squeezed my eyes shut and a chill ran through me at the thought that it could all end so quickly.

A soft laugh was his only reply, and then his lips brushed my throat again.

Slowly and methodically, they covered every inch of skin.

Sometimes his tongue would shoot out, making me shiver.

I caught my breath several times as it moved lower.

When his lips caressed the swelling of my chest, I grabbed my skirt, my body arching toward him of its own accord.

The flat of his tongue caressed the rise above the hem of my black satin bra, and the sensation of damp heat burned me.

He moved, put an arm on my abdomen and turned his head.

My nose buried in her hair.

It smelled a little like fresh lotion from after washing, and I exhaled with a sigh.

My concentration shifted when I felt his finger creep up the curve of my cleavage, plunging into the space between my breasts before sliding under the edge of the bra.

His tongue followed it, and a groan rose from the back of my throat.

My nipples were so hard they hurt.

If he just ...

My body twisted, urging him to go a little lower, where I wanted him.

Where I needed it.

When I moved my hand, literally trying to take matters into my own hands to ease the pain, he moved again and grabbed my arm, lifting it above my head.

He got up high enough to free my left arm from under him and linked it with my right arm.

Holding both wrists with his right hand, he lowered his mouth to my chest again and continued to worship my now-burning skin.

"Please ... oh please Harry ..." I murmured past the moans he drew from me.

"What do you want Deb?" His breath went through the bra barrier and made me hurt even more. "Tell me what you want."

"Oh ..." My mind was blurry, and I suddenly felt embarrassed again.

Why can't you just understand what I'm asking of you?

"This could be?" His fingers brushed the lower part of my chest through the dress and I groaned. "Yes, I think that's what you want."

He teased again, and finally his hand cupped my chest, gently squeezing.

His thumb brushed the nipple.

Even through the material of the bra, it sent shockwaves through my entire body.

"Oh God!"

My eyes snapped open and I held my breath, staring at the ceiling but seeing nothing, reveling in the fact that he had finally touched me where I needed him.

I gasped when he moved his hand up and slid a finger under the edge of my bra and swept it over and over directly over my nipple.

Heat rushed and pooled between my legs.

The world calmed down.

His lips brushed my ear, his breath burning and still making me shiver.

My breath caught as his hand slid deeper into my bra to cup me completely.

I felt his skin a little rough as he kneaded my breast, rolling my nipple between his thumb and his other fingers.

I turned to him, my mouth seeking his.

He groaned, pressed his lips to mine and pushed me onto my back again.

I moved under him, echoing his moan as his tongue swept my mouth and played with my tongue.

He squeezed my chest once more and then withdrew his hand.

He released my left wrist, slid his hand over my shoulder, and pulled both the strap of my dress and my bra down my arm.

Cold air brushed my now bare chest.

My nipple tightened painfully.

I was out of breath, shaking, when his fingers slid down my arm and slowly lifted it back above my head.

When I felt him tie something around my wrist, I automatically shook myself.

"Harry?"

"Yes, Debbie?" He came down kissing my arm and onto my chest, sucking my nipple into his mouth.

"Oh!" I forgot what I was going to ask him, my nerves cleared with that simple action, and I arched against him.

He chuckled, teasing my nipple with his tongue as he climbed on top of me and released my other wrist.

When he discovered my right breast, he moved his mouth to that side as he put that hand back on my head.

I struggled to swallow, watching him tie my right wrist.

"You're so sexy". Her eyes were sparkling as she sat next to me, staring at my bare chest, my dress and bra just below my bust.

I gently tugged on my wrists and swallowed the tension.

There was enough slack for my arms to relax against the pillows, but not enough to be able to untie me if I wanted to.

"I didn't think you would remember."

What had happened to my voice?

It sounded very hoarse.

"Oh, I remember. I remember everything."

That lazy smile, that deep tone, that sudden dark look in his eyes made my heart skip a beat.

My mind raced to remember everything we had discussed ... and I wondered if I had forgotten to mention something.

But I lost my concentration when he reached below my back, unhooked the clasps of my bra, and unzipped my dress.

I kept my eyes on him, seeing apparent fascination in his eyes as he shook my dress, revealing more and more of my naked body.

He held his breath when he revealed my black satin panties.

I walked over to him and he stopped, grabbing my hips and running his thumbs back and forth over my covered skin.

Resuming my nudity, the satin of my skirt brushed my bare legs, and then tossed the dress aside.

His fingers slid up my calves, up to my knees, and then down again to unbutton and remove my heels.

I had a sudden surge of anger.

I slowly ran the tip of my tongue along my upper lip and moved my hips.

"So you like what you see?"

His eyes shot up to mine, and I swear I saw a flash of fire in them.

He didn't speak, but he slid his fingers under the hem of my panties and slowly pulled them down.

I gulped, aware that I was really worried that he might like what he was seeing.

Cold air brushed against me, and I couldn't help pressing my thighs together, groaning and squirming as he just stared at me.

A couple of times, he raised his hand as if to touch me there, but his hand returned to his lap.

I wish I could read your mind.

He reached into his back pocket and then leaned toward me, brushing his lips against mine.

"Are you okay?"

I took a couple of deep breaths and then smiled.

"Yes, I'm OK."

His eyes met mine, and he smiled back.

"Liar."

His hands moved over my face.

A soft cloth covered my eyes, blocking the light, and secured the elastic band over my head.

My breath hitched.

I could not avoid it.

He was correct.

A part of me worried that I had gone too deep.

I had wanted this.

But once my control was gone, my nerves returned and I was scared.

Not necessarily Harry, but what he would do ... or not do.

It seemed to have done this before.

What if I don't live up to your expectations?

CHAPTER III

Which brought us back to me lying on the bed, completely naked, blindfolded and hands tied to the headboard.

Harry was sitting or standing in another part of the room listening to repetitions of Law and Order.

I very much doubted he was watching television.

I could really feel his eyes on me.

And it wasn't that uncomfortable feeling when you know someone is looking at you and wonder why and then nervously look around trying to locate the culprit.

Instead, I felt the heat spreading through me, glad that it found me worth looking at.

Several minutes passed, the series went to a commercial, and in the background, I heard the clear click of the hotel room door opening and closing.

"Harry?"

There was no answer.

I tried not to panic, but couldn't help but pull on my restraints.

I didn't hear anyone else in the room, which was a good thing.

But still...

My thoughts were getting over me when I heard the door open again.

I held my breath, heard the clink of ice in a glass and the hiss of a soda can opening.

The heat of another body brushed my right side, and the bed sagged under the weight of someone sitting.

I gasped when a cold palm brushed my right nipple.

"Did you miss me?"

I let out a ragged sigh, relieved to hear Harry's voice.

"Tell me something the next time you go!"

"I'm sorry. I didn't mean to scare you."

His lips brushed mine.

I smelled the tail on his breath.

Our tongues flirted for a moment, and then he leaned back.

"Should we start?"

I smiled, relaxing against the pillows.

I heard him put down his glass, and then he started rummaging under my head, lowering the comforter and blankets.

My skin prickled, going goose bumps, when his hands brushed against my body.

I helped as much as I could in my position by lifting my body.

When she was already lying alone on the cold sheets, the weight of the bed shifted again and the television went silent.

"You can't see anything, can you?"

I leaned my head forward, to both sides, and then relaxed again.

"No, nothing."

"Then enjoy. And not a word."

I nodded and flexed my wrists and fingers.

I knew he was looking at me again, and heat built between my legs.

I moved my hips, wiggled my toes, and then turned my ankles.

Anything to keep me distracted.

My lips were suddenly dry and I licked them, swallowing and finding my mouth dry as well.

I forced myself to breathe normally, listening for any hint of what she might be doing.

The air conditioning turned off, and then I only heard her even breathing.

But even so, it didn't touch me.

After several more minutes, my muscles relaxed and my legs opened slightly.

His breath caught and I smiled.

I was wondering if he was masturbating, but surely he would have heard some indication of that.

I was going to ask him if everything was okay when I felt it.

It was a very light touch, directly on both my nipples.

I groaned when they hardened.

The sensation moved downward, following the curve under my breasts and to the sides.

It was definitely a feather, the fullness brushing my skin like the softest fingertips.

It moved over my abdomen, outlining my ribs, circling my navel.

My hips jerked as the tip brushed against my groin area, where my leg joined my body.

I shuddered, cooing.

He repeated the movement, moving over my hip and slowly back again, following the line of my pelvis.

I was squirming when he ran the flat part of the feather across the top of my left thigh.

Goosebumps rose again and I spread my legs wider, using my feet to gain strength against the bed to push up.

Harry chuckled.

"Patience, Deb."

But he slid the feather along the inside of my thigh, down below my knee and calf.

I laughed when he tickled the bottom of my foot.

It was changed to work on my right side.

I could feel the heat of his body leaning over my legs.

The feather traced the same pattern on the other leg, but back.

From my foot to my calf, below my knee and over my thigh, through my pelvis and my ribs.

I arched my back and moaned softly as my nipples brushed against the rolled up sleeve of his shirt.

"Hey, don't cheat!"

I smiled and licked my lips, but I behaved and leaned back.

He pulled away and I felt him move over my head.

The feather traced the bottom of my right arm to my wrist and brushed my fingers.

He drew circles on my open palm before working his way down my arm again.

The tip swept across my shoulder, down my collarbone, and across my throat.

I leaned my head to the left against the pillow and sighed as he traced designs on my neck and teased my ear.

When he slid the pen under my chin, I tilted my head to the other side and sighed again as I repeated the same motions all over my neck, over my shoulder, and into my left arm and hand.

I moved my fingers, the pen sliding between them.

He stood up, letting my body beg.

My fingers clenched, echoing constrictions, deep within me.

I licked my lips again, feeling my heart pound.

Fortunately, it was not long gone.

A new sensation, I guess a silk scarf, brushed my fingertips and down both arms at the same time.

It covered my face, slowly sliding down my nose and mouth to cover my neck.

When he reached my breasts, I arched up, moaning.

He rubbed it back and forth over my sore nipples.

Then the handkerchief caressed my abdomen and hips, briefly brushing my pelvis on its way to my thighs and feet.

He repeated the process in reverse, careful to stop at the areas where he was moaning in pleasure.

And then the handkerchief was gone as fast as it appeared.

I heard Harry rummaging through a plastic bag, and then he was again lying on the bed next to me.

There was a click that sounded like a plastic cap.

I gasped when something cold covered my left breast.

His tongue licked my nipple before sucking it into his mouth.

"Ohh!" I arched into him, and he obeyed by dragging his tongue across my chest, his hand cupped and squeezing.

When he apparently licked my left breast, he moved to lie on my right side and repeat the process.

I could feel the heat throbbing inside me, begging to be touched, and I whimpered.

"I know, Deb. I know." He squeezed my right breast and reached out to kiss me, dipping his tongue into my mouth. "Mmm."

I tasted chocolate and moaned with it.

He kissed my chin and neck, stroking my shoulder.

A cold stream of chocolate fell on my lips, and I licked hungrily.

His finger pressed between my lips, and I sucked it deep into my mouth, wiping it of chocolate too.

Then coldness crept up my chin and throat.

It continued through the cleavage between my breasts and circled my navel.

His tongue and lips followed slowly, making me shiver with excitement.

The mattresses squeaked as he walked away, and then I heard running water in the bathroom.

He came back a minute later, slowly running a warm washcloth over my neck, my breasts, and my stomach.

The change in temperature made me gasp and my body rippled.

He lay on my left side again, his hand extended over my abdomen.

He massaged me for a moment, his mouth covering my left nipple, nibbling and sucking gently.

I tried to reach down to run my fingers through his hair, but my hands couldn't reach him, reminding me that I was contained.

I clung to the air instead, trying to press my side against him.

His hand slid up and cupped my chest.

I cried from the sudden bite of an ice cube rubbing against my nipple.

I pulled away, but there was nowhere to go.

Cold water dripped down my chest, ice slowly circling my nipple.

It hurt, but the sudden pain became numbingly pleasant and I felt the heat rise once more between my legs.

I whimpered, trying to pull away now, clenching my fists.

"Shh. Shh."

His free hand pressed against my stomach again, holding me against the bed as he sucked on my numb nipple, licking up the water.

He pulled away, and a warm towel covered my trembling chest.

I should have been ready for him to move onto my right breast, but the icy ice cube in him still amazed me.

I screamed, and once again, I was groaning and pulling away, regardless of his attempts to calm me down.

The sharp pain returned, squeezing my nipple, numbing the skin around it.

When the ice melted, his mouth licked and sucked up the water, and then the towel warmed my chest.

My head was blurry now.

I couldn't believe how excited she was, even more so since the ice treatment.

I felt a little guilty that I enjoyed the brief pain.

The resulting pleasure was amazing.

I was glad that Harry had tied my wrists.

She was sure she would have tried to stop him if she had the chance.

How long have we been at this, anyway?

My thoughts returned to the present when the ice slid between my breasts.

I screamed and arched.

Harry caught my sides in his hands, holding me against him as he dragged the ice up and down the center of my body with his mouth, my breasts brushing his cheeks.

I felt the water pool in my belly button, spilling over my hips.

I didn't think my body could stop shaking.

When the ice disappeared, his tongue replaced it, licking my skin that now sizzled under the cold layer of ice and water.

His hands moved to cup my breasts, squeezing them as he stroked the neckline in the middle.

It took me a moment to realize that he was lying between my legs.

Instantly I raised my knees to his hips.

He felt so good nestled against me where he most needed to be touched.

I sighed, at the heat of his hard bulge evident through his pants.

His deep laugh vibrated through my chest.

"Okay. I get the idea."

He released me and crawled away from my legs.

I complained at the sudden absence, but his hand on my hip calmed my twisted body.

His fingers worked their way between my curls and my hot skin.

I sighed.

My legs spread again.

One of his fingers pressed against my slick slit, briefly touching my clit.

I cooed, spreading my legs wider.

He slowly stroked his palm over my outer lips.

Every now and then, he would wet his finger, dragging it from one end to the other, making me gasp.

His hand stopped, cupping my mound, and two fingers pressed, spreading swollen lips.

I held my breath when his thumb circled my clit.

And then a finger slid lower.

He toyed with it, tracing the edge of my eager hole before moving to brush the walls of my inner lips.

My hips jerked, trying to force him down inside me already.

His free hand pressed my hips onto the bed, and then he was completely stroking my pussy.

The heel of his hand rested against my pelvic bone as his first three fingers slid down, down the valley, and snuggled up to brush my clit.

And again.

It was an exquisite feeling, finally getting him to touch me, easing the pressure I felt a bit.

My hands clenched, my body arching, struggling to free itself.

I groaned, throwing my head back onto the pillow as he pushed two thick fingers inside me and then sucked my nipple between my teeth.

His hand sped up, pressing hard and deep.

The tension in my belly increased, and I tightened my thighs around his hand, screaming.

His hand stopped, but his fingers kept moving, still buried between my legs.

He sucked on my chest as I rode toward my first climax.

When I caught my breath after cumming, he pulled away.

I heard him reaching into the bag again, and then he was lying between my legs, spreading my thighs.

My breathing hitched again when I felt something creamy and cold spread over my pussy.

I winced and sucked on my lower lip, unable to keep my hips from arching into him.

His fingers brushed the inside of my thighs, and then he pressed one finger, sliding it up and down my pussy.

I gulped and took a deep breath only for him to slide his finger into my mouth.

My lips closed around his finger.

I moaned at the taste of whipped cream with a hint of my own sexual juices.

As he sucked on her finger, he stroked it in and out, mimicking what he had already done downstairs before.

It wasn't hard to think of him doing that with more than just his fingers.

Just thinking about the fact that he had covered my pussy in whipped cream, and most likely guessing why, based on recent experience with chocolate, made me gasp.

He had already played with me more times than I could count.

And although I had already had many new experiences tonight, I never imagined a boy licking me down there.

I felt him sit on the bed, not touching me.

He growled, long and low.

It was the sexiest sound I'd ever heard, and I couldn't help but repeat it.

The bottom layer of the whipped cream was starting to melt and dripped around my clit.

I shifted, moaning softly when he pressed more whipped cream between my lips.

I had put shaving cream there before when I tried to shave my pussy, and the feeling was just as erotic now, squashing and caressing my sensitive skin.

"We're getting a bit fighter, aren't we?"

I made an unintelligible sound of impatience, and he laughed.

I loved his laugh as much as his sexy growl.

I struggled to swallow, loving what he was doing to me mentally and physically, despite my intermittent frustration.

Harry ran his fingers over my left breast, along the heavy curve below, over the gentle surf at the top, outlining the areola.

He cupped and massaged my chest.

His thumb and forefinger pinched my nipple.

I bit my lip to keep from screaming.

He gently rubbed the hard lump from side to side, then pressed his palm against it, easing the sharp pain.

His hand slid down the neckline in the middle and brushed my right breast.

His fingers touched me again, electrifying my skin, sending new fire between my legs.

When he pinched my nipple, I rolled over to him, willing him to put my mouth on it again.

"Very sensible."

His breath brushed my cheek, his tongue swept my jaw, and then he was making my wish come true.

His lips closed over my nipple and gently sucked in the sharp pain I'd created.

I rocked from side to side, groaning.

I felt the whipped cream stick to my thighs now, and I wondered if I'd forgotten.

I didn't want him to stop licking my chest, but suddenly I wanted him down.

I wanted to know what it felt like to have his tongue teasing me there, just as he was teasing my nipple.

What it would be like to have the tip of his tongue pressing inside me, his teeth biting my slick skin.

He ran the flat part of his tongue over my nipple again and then slid down my body, kissing and nibbling and licking every inch of my skin along the way.

Before long, he was lying between my legs.

He kissed my hips and then trailed his tongue across the junction between my legs and my pelvis.

He added a new layer of whipped cream, and then his arms wrapped under my thighs and parted.

I groaned, my body convulsed slightly.

I felt his hot breath against my soft curls.

I cried when his tongue came out and touched my clit.

I spread my legs wider and he lifted my naked pussy closer to his mouth.

His tongue licked at me again, and I groaned in relief.

His fingers massaged my thighs as he licked deeper along my pussy.

I heard the soft sound of his tongue licking the mixture of my moisture and the spread cream coating.

His tongue was everywhere, missing no crevices.

It was a slow and tortuous process, and I prayed it wouldn't stop soon.

I let go, my hips jerking under his mouth.

When he sucked on my clit, I screamed again.

When he pressed the tip of his tongue against me, I groaned.

I couldn't get enough of him.

And I wanted to touch him more than ever.

I cursed my restraints ... and they still raised the arousal level at the same time.

I have never had such a variety of feelings running through me at once.

I came a second time when his finger slipped inside me again.

He stroked me through my orgasm, his mouth still clinging to my clit, his hot breath mingling with my own warmth and wetness.

I was coming down from my climax when I felt the ice cube and screamed.

I had pushed him inside me, and cold water ran between my buttocks.

His fingers pressed, holding the ice in place, letting my heat melt it.

I felt my muscles tighten around his fingers, and he slowly stroked them in and out at the same time as my screams.

Another ice cube joined the scene, this time against my clit.

I fell into another orgasm, my head rolling back and forth between my raised arms, feeling the ice and his fingers caressing me.

His mouth licked my pussy again as I squirmed under him.

Somehow my fingers managed to grasp the pillow.

I think I yelled some curses because Harry chuckled and said something about me like 'you're a bad girl', the sound vibrating against my skin.

Finally, he offered me some relief and walked away, lowering my legs onto the bed.

I was panting, my eyes tight.

My body felt on fire, as if nothing I'd done so far had completely satisfied it, and yet I felt exhausted.

His mouth covered mine.

I managed to find the strength to kiss him back, tasting and smelling my own sweet musk on his lips.

CHAPTER IV

I must have fallen asleep, because my next thought was to wonder why I was lying face down on my stomach.

My wrists were still tied to the head of the bed, above my head.

I was still blindfolded and still naked, but I had turned around.

I sighed, feeling my breasts press against the warm sheet, my face nestled in a pillow that lay between my head and my arms.

He could reach the wooden slats at the headboard now.

I grabbed them lightly, smelling my sweat and perfume on the pillow.

I was about to call Harry when I felt warm liquid on my shoulder blades, and then the sensation of hands spreading the liquid over my skin.

It smelled of lavender.

"Welcome back Deb. You took a little nap." He leaned down and kissed my cheek. "I took advantage of the situation and repositioned you. Are you feeling okay? Do your arms hurt?"

I smiled and muttered:

"No, I'm fine".

"Well."

He kissed me again and then began to massage my back and shoulders.

His fingers slid over the skin due to the oil.

His hands gently pressed and tugged on my muscles, drawing moans and sighs from deep within me.

I had had several massages before, but none had been that sensual.

It turned me on more than it really eased any pent-up tension.

His fingers moved to the base of my head, massaging my scalp and behind my ears.

I breathed slowly, remembering where else those fingers had massaged me.

When he was done with my neck, he raised his arms to my hands.

Our fingers intertwined, stained with oil.

He squeezed my hands and came back down to my back and sides.

I shuddered when his fingers brushed my breasts, rubbing the oil around my chest where his fingers could reach.

I was groaning now, feeling the weight of his body between my legs, pressing against my ass.

I winced when I felt his bulge harden, but he stepped back, working my legs now.

I whimpered, burying my face into the pillow to muffle the sound.

He finished off my feet and slowly slid his hands down the back of my legs, over my butt, pressing along the back of my waist, hips, and down my sides.

His fingers brushed the sides of my breasts again, and then he lay on top of me, his mouth against my neck.

He brushed my hair back and nibbled on my right earlobe, making me moan.

I sighed and moved my ass against him, feeling his hardness throb in return.

She didn't want to beg, and had agreed not to say anything, but she was hot and uncomfortable despite the massage.

He needed more.

"Harry?" I whimpered and arched up again.

"Yes, Debbie?"

It sounded like fun.

As if waiting for this.

He pressed against me.

I growled.

"Please?"

He licked my neck.

"Please that?"

"Please..."

"Hmm?" He stood up, I heard the rustle of his clothes, and then sat next to me, his bare thigh against my shoulder.

His hand stroked my lower back, stroking my ass.

"What do you want Deb?"

I couldn't breathe for a moment, knowing his cock was there.

I whimpered and then bit my lower lip.

"Let me see."

He removed the blindfold and I had to blink several times to adjust to the light.

I noticed his bare shoulder and a barbed wire tattoo that encircled his left bicep.

My eyes moved downward, and I felt something deep inside me twist with desire when I saw his cock, hard and thick on her thigh.

He was pointing directly at me, his head bright red.

I held my breath and turned my face to the pillow, grasping the slats on the headboard again.

"That is all?" His hand moved lower, caressing the inside of my thighs.

I squirmed, groaning.

"No."

"What more do you want Deb?" His voice was softer, huskier.

I forced myself to swallow and closed my eyes.

"You. I want you. Please."

"A) Yes?" His fingers slipped through my wetness, rubbing against my clit.

I gasped, my eyes snapping open.
Somehow, I managed to find my voice again.

"I want more."

He stroked me slowly.
His fingers dug into me.

"A) Yes?"

"I want more."

I struggled to get my knees under me, spread my legs wider, and feel him deeper.

"How about this?" His voice was a hot whisper in my ear.

I whimpered when I felt him press his cock against me, stroking it back and forth between my outer lips.

"Oh please yes!"

"What do you want me to do next, Deb?"

My tongue froze.

I was just thinking dirty things in my head.

I had never imagined saying such words out loud.

Up to now.

But he couldn't say them.

I just couldn't ...

He leaned over my back, his cock resting between my buttocks, and whispered in my ear:

"Do you want me to fuck you Debbie? Do you want me to do it really slow?"

I choked and then nodded so furiously that my neck ached from the exertion.

He chuckled, sat back down and grabbed my left hip with his strong hand.

I felt him move his cock until it rested between my outer lips.

The pressure increased.

My whole body tensed.

She had played with toys many times, so she was used to the size of his cock.

But I had only imagined what it would be like to feel her real inside of me.

Despite being aroused and dilated, I was still worried about the pain.

He pushed my knees into his, and they slid even further on the sheets.

He pressed again, and this time he entered.

I choked again, burying my face into the pillow, pretending it was his fingers instead of his cock so I could relax.

And just as promised, very slowly, inch by inch, he entered my hot, wet pussy.

I couldn't believe the feeling.

There was no pain.

Instead, there was a strong, throbbing heat.

And pleasure.

Oh what a pleasure!

I thought it would never stop, and then it did, and we both stood very still.

"Are you okay Deb?"

One hand still held my hip

The other caressed the small of my back.

I managed to say "Yes".

He could only imagine our erotic scene: me on all fours, my wrists tied to the bed, my butt lifted towards him.

He knelt behind me, his cock buried deep inside me, his hands on my hips.

The tremors ran through me.

I had never imagined myself submissive ... until tonight.

He began to back away.

He made his way slowly, a little outside, back inside; He went out a little more, all the way back, until he slid so that only the head of his member remained inside.

It was an impressive experience, and I could only let out little gasps of pleasure as she moved.

His two hands gripped my hips now, and he slowly fucked me in and out, rocking my body back and forth against him.

He got into rhythm, and I found myself moving the same way of my own free will.

When he pushed all the way down, pausing for an extra deep thrust, burying his balls against my ass, I moaned louder.

I lost track of time, just enjoying the sensations:

His hands on my body.

His cock inside me.

The dull sound of him sliding into my pussy.

My heart was beating in my head.

Our heavy breathing.

I don't know if he said anything, but I was so focused on the growing pressure inside me that I don't think I would have heard him if he had.

He hadn't increased his speed at all times.

Thus the whole experience was intensified, the pleasure gained.

He shifted slightly, possibly to ease the pressure on his knees.

It didn't matter why he did it, but he also moved inside and I screamed, realizing that he had hit my G-spot.

He paused in his retreat.

"Debbie? Did I hurt you? Are you okay?"

"There!" Was all I could say, my breath caught in my throat, silently urging him to continue.

I grabbed the slats on the headboard and tried to push against him, but his hands stopped me.

He pushed forward, and I screamed when he hit him again.

"There!"

"Ah. Got it, Deb. Got it."

And he did.

Over and over again, he slipped deep into that perfect spot.

The edge was getting closer and closer.

And then I flipped over, screaming all the way.

I slumped back against the bed, but he continued to stroke, whispering words of encouragement.

He barely understood what he was saying, but his deep voice was comforting.

I felt his hands squeeze me tighter.

His hips slammed into my butt, a hot current entered me deep inside, I cried with him, and then we were still.

Surprisingly, he started stroking me again, as slow as before, and I got another orgasm.

As I shook under him, Harry reached up above me and untied my wrists.

I fell sideways.

He pulled me back against his chest, still inside me.

Tears came to my eyes when one of his hands covered my chest and caressed me.

His other hand fell to cup my mound, his fingers sliding between my thighs to rub my clit.

And I came for the fifth time.

At some point, I pulled his hands away.

I felt his cock slide out of me and lean against my leg.

He spread kisses along my shoulder blade and held me in the spoon position against him.

When I came back to reality and caught my breath, I turned around to look at him.

His arms wrapped around me and pulled me closer.

"We didn't use the hot tub," I murmured against his shoulder.

"What, not enough pleasure for one night?" He chuckled and pressed his lips to my forehead, brushing my hair behind my ear. "Check-out is not until noon tomorrow. So we have plenty of time."

I leaned my head back so I could look into his dark eyes.

They looked heavy, as sleepy as mine.

I managed to hide my yawn with a smile.

"Good, because I lack my revenge and I'm a bitch."

END

www.ingramcontent.com/pod-product-compliance
Lightning Source LLC
Chambersburg PA
CBHW020624160726
47991CB00002BA/928